THE CALL OF THE BLACK RIVER

A TALE FROM THE SPIRALS OF DANU

MARTIN ADIL-SMITH

ACCIPITER

The Accipiter Corporation

Published 2013 by The Accipiter Corporation
10 Abbey Park Place, Dunfermline, Fife, UK, KY12 7NZ

info@accipitercorp.com

ISBN: 978-0-9926964-1-2

Join "The Spirals of Danu" at the following social networks
www.facebook.com/spiralsofdanu
www.twitter.com/spiralsofdanu

Dedicated to all of those who have made this journey worth while

Tom & Sherrie
Andy
Rose
Jon
Röd
Fred
Adam & Emma
Jason

And the countless others.
Thank you.

Also by Martin Adil-Smith

The Demons of Emily Eldritch (short story)

A Gathering of Twine

Forthcoming titles in The Spirals of Danu series:

The Beggar of Beliefs

The Shackles of a Name

PROLOGUE

Where have all the Elders gone,
To battle against the odds?
Where are all the innocents,
To sacrifice to the gods?

"The Call of The Black River" by Even The Lost.
© G & L Tate 1978

Monday 15th August 1977 – Perkins Observatory, Delaware, Ohio.
The late afternoon sun flung its golden rays into the musty radio room where a young Jerry Ehman rocked back and forth on an uncomfortable plastic chair, trying to ignore the quiet chatter of the machines that surrounded him and concentrate on the latest wonder in this month's Penthouse Magazine.

His shift at the observatory was as it always had been. Sign in, read the handover notes... and wait.

The Big Horn Radio Telescope had been waiting fourteen years – since 1963 – for a signal from the vastness of space... for some sign of intelligence other than our own. And Jerry had grown bored of waiting.

He usually taught electrical engineering at Ohio State University, but his contract stipulated that, like all his colleagues, he must undertake one shift a month at the Perkins Observatory, which scanned the heavens for non-terran based radio signals as part of the Search for Extra –Terrestrial Intelligence.

Similar SETI projects like this had sprung up all over the world in the last twenty years, but even now there were mutterings in the dark recesses of academia that, despite the odds, Humanity was alone in the infinite ocean of space. The principle of the idea was that any civilization must take a similar technological route to space travel, and that would mean developing radio

5

So something, somewhere, must be broadcasting.

Except there was nothing but silence. The eternity that was the cosmos was like a cemetery on a misty winter's day; dead to all sound. No-one was listening, and Jerry believed that no-one was broadcasting simply because there was no-one out there to …

The chatter of the machines kicked up a gear, tearing Jerry away from the marvelous specimen of womanhood on page twenty-three. He looked from one monitor to another, and then to a third.

That's not right…

Swiveling around in his chair he picked up a printout as the normally quiet babble of the recording equipment became a hysterical cry, like that of a demanding child who had been told to go to bed. Jerry's eyes widened and his shocked mind tuned the noise out.

Sweet Jesus son of Mary…

There it was. In amongst all the background murmurings of the cosmos, there it was. Despite the warmth of the summer day, Jerry's arms goosed as his hairs raised themselves, like defiant Trojans making a final stand.

Jerry knew that there were protocols for this, but his mind was too shocked to react. For seventy-two ephemeral seconds The Big Horn Radio Telescope recorded the only extra-terrestrial radio broadcast known to Mankind.

Finally, after all this time…

It was all Jerry could do to pick up his pen and annotate the margin of the printout with a single word.

"Wow!"

CHAPTER 1

Sometime after midnight,
I hear a battle's melody,
Somewhere just beyond my reach,
There's something looking back at me.

"The Call of The Black River" by Even The Lost.
© G & L Tate 1978

Friday 16th December 1977 – Jenkins Residence, Lake of the Woods, Locust Grove, Virginia.

Tom Jenkins dreamt the same dream he had nearly every night for the last thirty-three years. It was 1944, he was twenty-two and the last illusions of his teenage years were being shredded as he was forcefully reminded that he was neither a young god, nor was he immortal.

He was back in his co-pilot's seat in 'Kismet's Reach' – a B-17 Flying Fortress that he and his crew had been told could out-fly and outgun any Nazi Messerschmitt. As they were now learning, that claim was not entirely accurate.

"Stay in formation," his headset crackled, the commander's voice tensing with the approaching shadows from the horizon. "Stay in formation."

Against the dark of the encroaching night, Tom could see dozens of silhouettes about him, as the convoy advanced across occupied Europe towards its target, deep in Nazi-held territory.

The young man felt the whole airframe shudder as the cannon in the underbelly ball turret pounded away at the approaching German squadron.

"They're coming round again Jimmy," Captain Gustafsson barked to the cannon operator.

"I got them," the headset replied.

"This is Green Leader... we have a second squadron inbound, I repeat we have a second... disregard message. We have two more squadrons inbound. Repeat, two more inbound. Look alive people."

"This is Green-Four. We have visual on a fourth squadron coming out of the sunset."

Tom looked to his Captain, tension and doubt etched onto his youthful face. "Where the hell is our support?"

Captain Gustafsson shrugged. "Don't worry. We're here to do our job. Keep her steady."

All around came the rough resonating rumble of the fifty caliber cannons, discharging hot leaden death into the twilight sky as the heavy bombers tried to repel the diving Messerschmitts. Their headsets crackled with information being relayed from one aircraft to another as the gunners tried to co-ordinate their attack against overwhelming enemy numbers.

"This is Green Three... we're hit... we're hit... we're..." The transmission ended in a burst of static, causing the youngest Jenkins boy to wince.

Even though Tom knew every crewmember on board Green Three, he allowed himself no moment of mourning. There was a mission to complete and the time for grieving would come once Berlin had fallen.

"Green Seventeen is down..."

"Green Twenty you got three of them on your... Jesus..."

"Green Nine you have an engine fire in the number four... cut the fuel... cut the..."

The ball turrets continued to pound away, sending tremor after tremor through the airframe, as though some prehistoric leviathan was trying to shake off millennia of earth and rise up.

"Stewart," Gustafsson snapped to his navigator. "Time to target?"

"At least two hours Sir."

The Captain muttered, "We're not going to last more than twenty minutes in this. Hank," he called to the squadron leader. "We've got to..."

"Agreed Fred. All units begin evasive maneuvers."

Tom took the yoke and began to bank the immense craft, knowing he was exposing his turret gunner to the oncoming enemy assault the way a surrendering antelope yields its soft underbelly to the lion, but betting that it would give Jimmy enough time to pick off a few more sonsof...

"There's too many," their gunner's voice crackled.

"We can't abort," Gustafsson replied, his voice remaining level and even.

"This is Green Twenty... we're..." The sound of another explosion rippled through air as the Messerschmitts once again charged through the bomber formation like Black-Backed Jackals tearing through a pack of frantic warthogs.

Kismet's Reach lurched and warning lights began to flash across the dashboard as the wail of the klaxon penetrated the concentration of the cockpit crew.

"They got the number one engine… cutting the fuel."

Looking out to the port side, Tom saw the propeller slow to a stop and the choking caustic smoke faded into the bullet-filled air. Against the dying sun, it looked as if a mighty beast of the sky was hemorrhaging black blood.

Gustafsson shook his head as he rapidly reasoned through the options. "Stick her on the deck." he said quickly

"Captain?" Tom replied.

"It'll be our only chance. I'm betting that they won't follow a lone kite down – they'll focus on the pack… and even if they do, they'll lose us against the canopy of the Teutoburg Forest. Let's put her on the deck."

Both men pushed their controls forward, dipping the nose of the mighty aircraft.

"Captain!" Jimmy screamed. "There's another squadron coming… oh Jesus…"

Bullets ripped through the hull, strafing the ball turret and the navigation equipment. Sparks flew across the fume-filled interior and a myriad of red lights lit up the cockpit. Smoke forced its way into Tom's mouth as he tried to breathe and the acrid taste made him want to puke.

"They got the number three engine… cut the fuel…"

The klaxon began to sound again, louder and more insistently, filling Tom's young head.

*

Tom thrashed wildly, throwing the heavy duvet from his sweat-soaked body, as the warning klaxon became the sound of the ringing telephone.

A bedside lamp came on and Sherrie picked up the receiver.

"Yes?" his wife asked blearily through a fog of sleep. "Yes sir," her voice snapped to full wakefulness. "Yes sir. I understand… No sir, he is right here… We'll be no more than an hour."

Tom began to pull himself up, his aching back reminding him that at fifty-five, he needed to slow down a little. He looked first to the red LED alarm clock which glowered at him menacingly, informing him that it was a little after three, and then questioningly at Sherrie.

Sherrie returned the receiver to its cradle and got out of bed. "That was The Administrator. We're being called in."

Administrator Robert Frosch was the head of NASA, and Tom came to full wakefulness. "Did he say why?" he asked, getting out of bed and making a point of ignoring his prominent paunch – he knew he needed to work on that, and he had promised Sherrie countless times in the last few months that he would watch his health.

Sherrie pulled her nightie off and reached into the wardrobe for a fresh blouse. "They have a confirmed contact."

*

The Jenkins' black sedan sped along Interstate 95 like a lone horseman desperately galloping for some distant sanctuary. Tom's foot pressed the accelerator to the floor and they were making good time to Washington. He had thrown off the last vestiges of his nightmare with a quick coffee that scalded his lips before they had left their house, and now they traveled in silence as his mind mulled over The Administrator's message.

The radio presenter was giving an update on a series of grisly murders that had taken place in the last few months. The latest was a middle-aged man who had been found in so many pieces that it was only from his discarded wallet that he had been identified – Jason Parrot. Despite being lost in his own thoughts, there was a flicker of recognition deep within Tom. He had gone to school with a boy of the same name. Of course it was probably just a coincidence, and it had been nearly forty years since he had seen many of his fellow students. He had kept in touch with his best friend – Adam Cannon – for a little longer, but even so it had been at least two decades since he had heard from him.

Every time he thought about his old school friends, it brought back that night… the Indian girl screaming… the fire… and …

The radio presenter moved on to the next article, speculating on the health of Charlie Chaplin, before giving a favorable review of Travolta's new film, *Saturday Night Fever*. Debbie Boone began singing *You Light Up My Life*… and Tom did not hear a single word.

Confirmed contact.

It had only been a few months since that fool Ehman had recorded the now infamous 'Wow!' signal. That radio transmission had been a terrestrial signal bouncing off some low orbiting space junk, but that had not stopped the world's media descending into a fit of fervor.

"Never let the truth get in the way of a good story son," his father had told him wryly many years ago. Old Man Jenkins had been a hack in Tom's home town of Lorain, Ohio. The twenties had been good but, like everywhere else, the thirties had been hard and, when war had engulfed Europe, Tom had been one of the first of his class to sign up to the USAF.

In truth he had been glad to leave. The town was sharply divided into the new generation of white collar workers, and the families of farmers who had worked the land since the first settlers had arrived. Tom was in the former category and both he and his school friends had looked at the barn children – known as Barnies – with disdain. Even by the age of ten, their skin was tanned to leather, and their crooked teeth and lank arms made him feel queasy. Plus they spent too much time with Indian children, and Tom's father had warned his two sons against the heresy of mingling with such creatures; they weren't God Fearing like honest folk, and their pagan ways made them little more than animals.

The war, for all its grief and hardship, had allowed Tom to get away from the heathen savagery that he felt infected Lorain. In the USAF there was discipline and order and the bible... good things that a man could rely on.

When peace finally broke out, Tom had returned to a changed America. Instead of joining his friends as they transferred to The First Civilian Division, Tom stayed with the Air Force and had been sponsored on part-time courses in aviation, aeronautics, and finally engineering. He had been critical in securing The Groom Lake facility and, when NASA was formed in 1958, he found the offer of secondment too tempting to refuse.

His role had been leading the Communication Development Team, which was grander than it sounded and focused more on encryption than it did new technologies. Still, as the discipline had progressed and more became known about the cosmos, the question of life beyond our solar system had become increasingly pressing and, when the Agency had begun their own SETI program in 1971, Tom was the obvious choice to head the new division.

That did not mean it had all been plain sailing – far from it. Despite new patents coming out of his department on an almost monthly basis, Congress was unhappy with the lack of results and now Senator Proxmire was leading an inquiry into whether the department should continue to be funded, or whether the budget should be diverted to 'more deserving programs.'

Ehman's discovery in August had taken the pressure off for a few weeks but, when the signal was shown to have an Earthly origin, the calls for cuts had begun again. And now this.

Confirmed contact.

Tom drummed his fingers on the steering wheel absently and Sherrie looked across to him, smiling. "What are you thinking?" she asked, the dashboard lights catching the fine freckles on her narrow face that Tom had found attractive so many years ago, and still did today.

Her husband shrugged but made no reply.

She smiled knowingly to herself – he was playing his usual game of never wanting to give anything away, but wanting to be drawn out. By contrast the glow of the lights reflected on her husband's meaty jowls giving him a haunted look, and the darkness of the early morning hid the prominent gray of his otherwise dark closely cropped hair.

"Oh come on," she said. "I know you better than that. Spill."

Tom looked at her through the corner of his eye and returned the smile. "Same old. Ehman. Proxmire. Those fools in Congress."

Tom and Sherrie had met just after they both joined NASA in 1958 – only a month after Tom's long term girlfriend, Richelle Dawkins, had split up with him - and they had married a year later. Sherrie was a few years out of Caltech, and was a statistician turned mathematical modeler. She had followed her husband into the SETI program where she now made recommendations on which areas of space should be scanned, based on the likelihood of life-bearing planets. She too had been born in Ohio, but a few years after Tom, and she had been mostly raised in the plains of North Ridgeville. They had never met in their youth, but when fate interceded to bring them together they found that they knew many of the same people, and it was this shared history that had sealed their union.

"Which is it?" she asked, pulling her suit jacket around her. Tom always insisted on driving with the air conditioning on, claiming it helped him stay alert, regardless of the weather outside.

"What do you mean?"

"Which is it you're thinking about? Ehman? Proxmire? Or Congress?"

Tom gave in. "Ehman," he replied, looking back to the road. There were pockets of freezing fog that obscured the road completely, and the cold December morning had left a thin sheen of frost on the tarmac river. Thankfully there was no snow, and in a few hours there would be enough passing traffic to break up the patches of ice, but for now he was mindful of both the pressing need to get to DC, and the risk of skidding.

"Ah. You think there was something in his signal after all?"

Tom shook his head and chewed his bottom lip before answering. "I don't know. I *do* know that I don't want them to send me back to Delaware."

The Perkins Observatory, Delaware had been the scene of more of Tom's failures than he cared to admit. In the fifties he had returned there for a part-time course in aeronautics, sponsored by the USAF, and promptly failed his first year, putting his entire career in doubt. It was only the intervention of his older brother, Joel, and his long time mentor, Professor Rooksby, who both lectured in engineering, that saved him from being kicked out of both Ohio State University and the USAF.

In sixty-three, Tom had returned to the university as the prodigal son to complete his doctoral thesis, and it was during this time that he had witnessed his brother's final downfall. Joel had been an infantryman during The War and, although he only spoke about it when he was drunk, he had seen the horrors of the concentration camp at Wewelsberg. Over the following two decades, those terrible images had replayed over and over again, wearing the older Jenkins boy down, until one day he snapped, hauled a loud mouthed long haired student out from the lecture hall and had beaten him to a bloody pulp on the campus lawn before he could be pulled off.

And Tom had seen it all. In the ensuing investigation, Tom gave an honest account of what he had witnessed. Joel was summarily dismissed and never forgave his younger brother. The two had not spoken since, not even at their father's funeral in sixty-nine.

Then there was Doctor Ehman and the 'Wow!' signal. The Delaware observatory was, for all intents and purposes, an adjunct of Ohio University, and Tom could still see the expression on the Dean's face as he told him that the signal was terrestrial.

He knew what it meant.

If it had been genuine, the university would have received more funding than it would have known what to do with. Instead, Doctor Ehman was singled out in the ensuing investigation into the debacle, for not having followed protocol. Dean Ballantine had just looked at Tom as if to say, *We've given you so much Tom, but you keep letting us down.*

Someday, those debts would have to be paid.

"I wouldn't worry about it," Sherrie said, rubbing her husband's arm reassuringly. "The Administrator is saying that the contact is confirmed. If they send you back to Ohio, I'm sure it'll be good for you."

*

Tom and Sherrie knew room 23W too well. The sterile meeting room, with its whitewashed walls on which hung an assortment of trite motivational posters, and gray plastic table and matching chairs, was their department's main conference facility. Tom and Sherrie stood around the water cooler waiting for The Administrator to appear. Rose Santiago, the department's principal astronomer, and Sherrie's best friend, had joined them a few minutes after they had arrived, still adjusting her grey pant-suit as she had walked in.

Rose had joined NASA straight out of MIT in sixty-seven, at a time when all of her contemporaries were tuning in and dropping out in The Summer of Love. Keen to appeal to the younger demographic, Tom had gone along with the agency's unofficial policy of positive discrimination, but when he met Rose for the first time, he knew that she was his preferred candidate. There was something about her that called out to him... not in a sexual way, but one that said that she belonged in his team. All of his division belonged together – that was the way it was. They had their mission, but they were family too.

Despite his years of training, Tom had learned to go with his gut on many things, and it had never let him down. Rose had been good for Sherrie, and that meant that they were good for the wider team.

The two women were deep in conversation about the meaning of The Administrator's message and Tom, who was never one for idle conjecture, had moved off to gaze out of the window as he waited for Administrator Frosch to appear.

He was so lost in his own thoughts that he barely heard the whisper.

"*…you must remember.*"

"Hun?" he said, turning from the window to Sherrie and Rose.

His wife looked at him expectantly with her large blue eyes, but said nothing.

Tom persisted. "Did you say something?"

Sherrie shook her head. "We were just talking about The Administrator's phone call."

Tom frowned. "Did you just tell me to remember something?"

"We were just remembering Ehman's signal…"

Tom nodded without further comment and turned back to the window, trying to put that fiasco from his mind. It was still dark outside and he could not see beyond the campus boundary which was lined with willows, silhouetted by the orange glow of the sodium streetlights. Thin tendrils of an early winter mist worked their way around the gnarled trunks and, out across the walkways, the grounds maintenance team had already begun their daily duties.

Abruptly the door opened, snapping Tom from his reverie and making him jump. Administrator Robert Frosch entered, followed by two other men. Robert was a few years younger than Tom, but had enjoyed a stellar career. Nearly fifty, he carried his extra weight on his face and waist, and he was bald with a few wispy strands of graying hair on the side. His powder blue eyes, although weary, shone from behind his thick-rimmed brown plastic glasses that accentuated his heavy features.

Tom did not recognize the second man – a wiry youngster no older than twenty-five, who sported a regulation buzz cut and wore an impeccably ironed dark suit and matching tie. His gait seemed almost mechanical – it was far too regular, and Tom guessed that he was Secret Service. He was used to seeing other agencies about the campus, but he had never before had one of their ilk in his meeting.

The third man caused a flicker of recognition in Tom. He had met him before somewhere… his mind tried to place him. He was something in radio physics… maybe at Cornell. He was early forties, with a full head of glossy hair and the thin lines on his round face told of a flamboyant laugh. His mind reached for a name. Carl… Carl something or other…

"Tom, Sherrie, Rose," Robert said, taking each of their hands and shaking it with his clammy own. "Thank you for coming at such short notice. I'm sorry for hauling you all in like this but… but we have a situation developing. Tom, I think you've met Dr Sagan before…"

Carl Sagan, that was it. Tom nodded perfunctorily to the plaid suited man.

"… and this is Agent Conrad Reid," The Administrator continued.

Tom and Sherrie exchanged questioning glances. "Agent?" Tom asked. NASA was supposed to be a civilian operation, although it was heavily populated with secondees from the various forces. That said, there had always been a clear emphasis to protect the image of the agency as a non-military institution. Even when another agency was on campus, they were expected to keep a low profile.

"Yes Tom, Agent," Robert looked at him as if daring him to challenge the man's involvement. "Now, if you would all like to take a seat, we'll begin the briefing."

For The Administrator of NASA to chair a SETI briefing was unheard of, and Tom had assumed that Robert would leave after the introductions had been made. Yet this did not prevent him challenging his manager immediately.

"Hang on a minute Robert, the rest of my team aren't here," Tom said to The Administrator. "There's Andrew Tong and Thorn and…"

"They've not been called in. This isn't a NASA meeting Tom," Robert interrupted. "If you sit down, Agent Reid will explain everything."

Tom went to say something more but Sherrie took him gently by the arm and guided him to his seat. She knew how her husband could get bent out of shape when he did not understand everything immediately.

The three NASA staff sat down without further protest and Agent Reid began passing thin beige files around for them to read.

"You'll all be familiar with the so-called 'Wow' episode in August of this year," the Agent began, his clipped accent revealing his New England heritage. "Since then we have spent a considerable amount of time analyzing the data…"

Tom leaned forward before Sherrie could stop him. "And who is 'we'?" The Administrator shot him a glare but Tom did not back down.

Reid looked at him and then answered slowly. "Professor Jenkins, I am a special agent of The National Security Agency on attachment to the United States Air Force…"

"If you're Air Force young man," Tom riled, "then you will address me first as Lieutenant Colonel, and then as Sir, do I make myself crystal clear?"

Reid did not balk at the angry older man and remained placid. "Yes Lieutenant Colonel. Do I have your permission to continue Sir?"

Tom grunted an acknowledgement and leaned back in his seat. This was the reason that he had never gone for Robert's job. Too many secret whispers, too much hand-shaking and too many political deals with other agencies. He just wanted to get the job done.

"Thank you Sir. We've spent the last five months analyzing the data from the 'Wow' signal. You will all be aware that it was determined to be terrestrial, albeit because it bounced off some low orbiting space debris it had the appearance of being extra-solar in origin. What has recently been determined is that, whilst the signal originated on Earth, it was alien in nature."

Silence descended over the room and the already charged atmosphere became increasingly tense. Even the usually cheery looking Carl Sagan now looked pale and drawn.

Rose shook her head, not understanding Reid's revelation. "What... what does that mean?"

Tom answered before the Agent, his voice low and weighed down by the gravity of the situation. "At the very least it means that someone on Earth has access to extra-terrestrial technology."

Reid was still standing. "Sir, if I may?"

Tom nodded.

"Ms Santiago, there are a number of scenarios that we are working up at the moment. You will appreciate that this is a fluid situation and as more information becomes available our parameters are modified. With what we know at the moment... one scenario is as Lieutenant Colonel Jenkins has said; someone has either direct access to alien technology, or has enough of an understanding to cobble something together.

"A second possibility is that there is non-terrestrial life on Earth and... and it is calling out to... to whatever is out there."

Tom's graying eyebrows knitted together in a frown. "What are we talking about here? Invasion?"

Reid shook his head. "Unknown Sir. We have been unable to decipher the transmission. It looks like it was just blind luck that Professor Ehman caught as much as he did. It could be a distress call or... something worse."

Sherrie considered all of what had been said, but could still not see why she and Tom had been called in, much less Rose. "Agent Reid, forgive me. I understand the urgency of this matter... but why are *we* here?"

Agent Reid looked to The Administrator for permission to continue, and received a silent nod of assent. "Dr Jenkins, ma'am... you are all here because you have the necessary security clearance to hear what I am about to say. In addition, your unique combination of skills and your existing relationships with each other means that, as a team, you all do not need to go through the normal bonding process.

"The Lieutenant Colonel... Professor Jenkins, knows every policy and procedure relating to extra-terrestrial contact. His standing within the USAF also makes him qualified to make threat assessments. You, Dr Jenkins, have degrees in astronomy and physics. If we do encounter something... the most likely language we'll be able to communicate in will be mathematics.

"Dr Santiago's understanding of planet hunting, combined with Dr Sagan's expertise in radio communication and exo-biology, make you ideal candidates for assessing and communicating with any life-form we encounter."

Tom could sense that Agent Reid was holding back. "What about you?" he asked.

16

The Administrator looked to the Lieutenant Colonel. "He's in charge of the operation Tom... that comes direct from The President."

Tom's anger physically choked him and he felt himself flush. Reid was a kid... no more than a year or two out of Langley. There was simply no way that this punk was qualified to...

Rose's soft voice cut through his red mist. "I'm sorry Agent, but you said 'operation'. What...?" she trailed off as The Administrator and Reid exchanged another glance that spoke of an already pressing situation was about to be revealed as being far murkier.

Reid adjusted his jacket, cleared his throat, and began. "Dr Santiago, we have located the area where the radio transmission originated... and it's still broadcasting."

Tom's anger went up another gear. "What? Why wasn't I informed?" he thundered.

The Administrator spoke quietly, trying to defuse the situation and win Jenkins round. "Tom... it was a Presidential decision. Christ, I only found out three hours ago. This whole thing... it's being contained. The fewer people who know the better... at least until we can get a handle on... on whatever it is."

"Fine," Tom spat, and then turned to Reid. "So where is the broadcast location?"

Even before The Agent replied, Tom knew. Reid took a second too long to respond, and he did not meet the Lieutenant Colonel's eye... and Tom knew.

"Sir, the broadcast is... it begins a new cycle every twenty-three hours, broadcasts for a few minutes and then cuts out. That's why it has taken us so long..."

"The location, Agent," Tom was insistent, already certain of the answer.

Reid looked down to his file and then back to Tom. For a moment Tom thought the hint of a smile played on the younger man's face. "Sir... it's Lorain, Ohio."

Sherrie brought her hands to her mouth and Rose gasped, looking first to her friend and then to Tom.

Tom grimaced and nodded, more to himself than anyone else. "Is this a joke?" his voice was even.

"No Sir," Reid replied.

"My home town?"

"Yes Sir."

"That's one heck of coincidence, isn't it Agent?"

Carl, Robert and Sherrie watched the sparring match between Tom and Reid, each sure that the older man was finally going to snap and strike out at the youngster, as his brother had done so many years ago.

"I don't believe in coincidences, Sir."

"Neither do I."

Silence returned and Rose crossed to the water-cooler to refill her plastic cup. "If you know where this thing is Agent," she began, "why the need to get us all up in the middle of the night? Why not secure the site and bring us in when we've had a full night's sleep."

Reid looked uncomfortable. "There is a… a complicating factor. The NSA didn't actually trace the source of the transmission, although we have verified it…"

"Agent, who traced it?" Tom interrupted.

The Agent shifted his weight, his awkwardness revealing his youth. When he spoke, his voice was nearly a whisper. "Spetsbureau Thirteen."

Tom found himself smiling. "Do you want me to tell them all what that is, or will you do it?"

Reid looked first to Carl, and then to Rose and Sherrie. "Spets Thirteen… it's a specialist division of the KGB. We intercepted a message intended for them, nearly five hours ago. We suspected that the Soviets would be carrying out their own investigation into 'Wow'… but we had no idea that they were so much further along than us. We simply don't have time to assemble our own squad – that's why we need you."

"Agent… you've told my team who Spets Thirteen is. Now tell them *what* they are," Tom interjected.

"Spets Thirteen," Reid began reluctantly, "is known as the Department of Wet Affairs. They are a kill team. If we don't get to this thing before they do, they will either bring it over to their side or destroy it. We really don't have much time."

*

The winter air was crisp and Tom watched various pieces of equipment that his team had requested being loaded onto a van. It would be a short drive to Dulles Airport and then an hour flight to Lorain County. They could have flown straight into Hopkins, but that was a bigger airport with stricter adherence to procedures. Lorain County Aerodrome… it was barely a dirt strip with a wooden control tower and one of the old pre-fabricated huts that served to welcome its infrequent users. They would be on the road within five minutes of landing.

Tom turned and met Robert's eye. The Administrator was staring at him and, since the meeting had broken up, there had been an uneasy silence between the two men.

"You could've handled it better in there," Robert muttered, lighting a cigarette, taking a draw, and then exhaling a billowing curtain of smoke into the cold morning.

"I would've done if it hadn't felt like an ambush," Tom retorted hotly.

Robert shook his head and took another draw. "Tom, no-one is trying to take SETI away from you…"

"Tell that to Proxmire." Tom knew he was trying to score points in a game he could never win.

Robert shrugged. "That's always been your problem. You always think that everyone is out to get you. You should take a leaf out of Rose's book."

The Administrator nodded to where Rose and Carl stood in deep conversation. The more time Tom spent around him the more he remembered – various conferences and expos. But the man had always been on the fringe. Sure he was charismatic, but he was not a big hitter.

"See," Robert continued. "She's taking a bit of time with him… she'll have a laugh and joke, get him to relax… maybe find out something interesting. And then, if she's the colleague you think that she is, she'll tell you. But you make it hard work Tom, you really do."

"Do I?" Tom's voice held a hint of bitterness.

"You know you do. You're so… so obsessed with keeping hold of everything that you've worked for that you never see the bigger picture."

Tom frowned. "What's that supposed to mean?"

"Oh come on," Robert replied, inhaling from his cigarette again. "We don't need to play this game. You wanted my job, but you didn't put in for it because you knew you'd never get it. You never appreciate that there is anything beyond your department… or the Agency. Even now you can't see the opportunity that has been handed to you."

Robert's words had stung Tom, but he pretended not to care. "I don't follow," he replied.

"You want me to spell it out for you? Fine. This operation… you have nothing to lose and everything to gain, but you're stomping your foot like a spoilt child because you're not in charge. Look at the scenarios; if you get to Lorain and there is nothing there, then it's the NSA's fault for badly translating the Spets message. If the Soviets get there before you or the mission goes bad, then it's Reid's fault – he's the one in charge. But if you get there and find something then… then *you're* the hero. It's *your* team. Reid can't appear on the cover of Time Magazine – he's a spook – but *you* can. Cheer up Tom, this'll be good for you."

Robert slapped the older man on the shoulder, turned back into the garage and made his way up the flight of concrete steps in the main building. Sherrie was still on the first floor collecting instruments and Tom could see that Reid had joined Rose and Carl.

Across the lawn, the freezing fog was beginning to lift, and the previously wraith-like forms of the grounds maintenance team began to gain substance.

"Good morning Professor," one of them said to him.

"Hey Gershom. How are you?" Tom replied. Gershom Eldritch had been on the facilities team since before Tom had joined the campus and although the man had to be pushing sixty, he looked thirty if a day. Tom put it down to simple living and working outside. He had always felt a kindred spirit with Gershom, and it was more than his countenance that so reminded Tom of the kindly German farmer who had rescued him from his crashed bomber and nursed him back to health.

"I'm just fine Professor. It's my last day today."

"I heard. New Mexico isn't it?"

"That's right sir. I got myself a fine role at the university in Valencia... and I'm hoping that there might be a girl waiting for me."

Tom chuckled, silently praying that it wouldn't be a Barnie-Woman. "Well good luck to you, although it seems a little harsh they have you working so early on your last day."

Gershom shrugged. "There's no let up Sir."

"Let up? On what?"

Gershom beckoned him to the side of the walkway and raked the ground. The frosted grass parted, revealing fresh green tendrils that criss-crossed the frozen earth like a finely interwoven mesh.

"Creeping Crowsfoot," Gershom muttered, and spat on the exposed vines. "The whole campus is riddled with it. It's an invasive species Sir. It's everywhere... all around you. You could walk by and never even know it was there. We just can't seem to ever get rid of the damned things."

Tom could see that the Crowsfoot would not be good for the lawns, but did not understand why so many men had been assigned to raking them up and at such an early hour.

Gershom saw his confusion. "Here," he said, and raked the lawn again, this time where the grass met the building.

Tom was shocked to see nearly half a dozen tendrils not just beginning to climb the red brick wall, but in places they had actually begun to burrow into the mortar.

"C Block has it worst," Gershom went on. "It's got in and started to blow the plaster. Bricks are spalling and the gutters are completely choked up. The Facilities Director has got everyone working overtime."

"But why when it's still dark?" Tom pressed, his interest piqued.

Gershom knelt down, twisted a closed bud from a tendril, and presented it to Tom.

"It's a buttercup," Tom said, as he unfurled the protective leaves and gazed upon the heavy yellow petals.

"Uh-huh. A wild variety I think," Gershom replied. "They open up during the day... feed the roots or something. But we only make progress against it at night. If we try during the day... why, it's like trying to staple water to a tree."

At that moment there was a shout, and Tom turned to see Sherrie beckoning him over. The van was loaded and it was time to go.

"That's my ride," Tom said turning back to Gershom. "Good luck in New Mexico… I really hope it works out with that girl."

Gershom smiled and shook Tom's hand. "Thank you Professor… I'm sure it will."

CHAPTER 2

Up where the stars meet the forests,
Out where the darkness hides the sea,
I could swear that there's something
Looking back at me.

"The Call of The Black River" by Even The Lost.
© G & L Tate 1978

Tom had always had the uncanny ability to fall asleep whenever and wherever he wanted. It was still too early for the notorious Washington rush-hour traffic, and their drive to Dulles had been uneventful. Even before the private Lear Jet had left the runway, Tom had reclined his seat and drifted off in a bid to catch up on his disturbed night's sleep.

Too quickly, his dream returned.

Kismet's Reach was racing over the verdant canopy of oaks and pines, silhouetting against the dusky sky, and trailing thick black smoke from two of its crippled engines as it desperately tried to outrun the approaching Messerschmitts. From the cracked cockpit window, Tom could see the battle raging above him as flashes and explosions rippled through the clouds, and too frequently recognizable chunks of a B-17 rained down, like a falling titan who believed that he had the strength to challenge Zeus only to discover too late the true meaning of power.

Jimmy – their gunner – was hurt but still able to operate the ball turret. However, both the navigator and radio operator were dead. The airframe shook again as the dual cannons pounded away at the advancing enemy, and the scream of the two remaining engines nearly drowned out all other noise as the Flying Fortress desperately tried to flee their pursuers.

"You've gotta take them out Jimmy," Gustafsson barked into his headset. "Let us open a gap between the pack... then we can make a break for it."

"Captain..." Tom's voice was filled with the fear of approaching doom.

Gustafsson did not need to ask what it was. He followed Tom's line of sight and saw the black bodies of three more Messerschmitts coming from the starboard side.

"Take her hard to port," he commanded, desperately trying to keep any hint of fear out of his voice, and failing.

"Captain, we can't outrun them... we've only two engines left and we're pissing fuel and oil every... She's done Captain. It's over."

Gustafsson looked to his younger co-pilot, resignation chiseled on to his face like a sepulcher's dedication. "Fine. We can't go back up and eject," he rolled his eyes skywards. "We'd be sitting ducks for them."

Tom's tone neared hysteria. "What else can we do?"

Gustafsson looked out of his window, trying to judge the horizon. "We can't be far from the North Sea. We'll put her down there... if we see a lake or something before, then we'll try our luck..."

His voice tailed off and Tom helped him bank the crippled aircraft. For nearly half an hour they stayed ahead of the pack of enemy fighters, and then, with only minutes to go before they met they coast, another horde fell upon them.

Bullets slammed through the hull, and the cannon in the ball turret stopped firing. Tom did not ask for Jimmy over the headset, knowing that his friend was already gone.

"Set the flaps," Gustafsson said. "Try and slow her down before we hit the ..."

Another volley strafed the stricken bomber, and this time Tom saw the sleek outline of their attacker pass over them... and bank for another run. Behind him, sparks fizzed and hissed as the radio and navigation equipment caught fire.

Instinctively Tom thought to put it out – fire was lethal in such a confined space – and then chided himself that such a reflexive action was pointless. They were going down any way.

"Tom..." Gustafsson rested back in his chair and looked to him, black blood bubbling from his lips, and the young co-pilot realized that his captain had been hit. Already his face was paling, and a dark stain was spreading across his jacket. Tom guessed that whatever had entered him – bullet or shrapnel – had come in through the back of his chair.

Tom took full control of the stricken craft. The sky had become like slate and the land abruptly gave way to the roiling black waters of the North Sea.

23

From high above, Tom could hear the Messerschmitts beginning their final attack run. The sound of the wind against the hull was like thunder as he angled the nose towards the ocean and braced himself for impact.

The force of Kismet's Reach striking the churning surface was like a concussion grenade going off in what little remained of the cockpit. A wall of water rose up, flooding the cabin and engulfed Tom, who looked to see if Gustafsson could yet be saved and knew that he could not.

All around came the shriek of tearing metal as opposing forces slammed into each other, and Tom could have sworn that the Captain had a thin smile upon his face as Kismet's Reach bore down into the cold inky depths like some avenging angel confronting the blackest gates of Hell.

And there, in a darkness so complete that Tom could not have believed it possible, he saw something reach out from the deep.

*

The sound of Kismet's Reach breaking apart became that of the Lear Jet's screaming engines at it touched down at Lorain County Aerodrome. The thin light of the winter sun trickled across the small landing strip, casting a wan glow upon everything. It had come a long way since Tom had last seen it, but it was like comparing a pea shooter to a ball turret; there was no comparison to the bigger regional hubs.

At some point in the last few years the runway had been resurfaced and the prefabricated hut that had been used as a mini terminal had been replaced with a brick building. Yet that was as far as any investment had gone. The gutters of the new 'terminal' were already choked with moss and tendril-like weeds, causing dark stains to run down the walls, and the grass along the fence line was long and unkempt.

Patches of snow littered the ground like discarded polystyrene and, as the team disembarked, their collective breath billowed like an obsolete steam engine that had not heeded the call that its time was over.

Tom had forgotten how cold it could get in his home town. A menacing breeze promised a storm in a day or two, and an icy breath blew from nearby Lake Erie, pushing the damp brumal air into his ageing joints. His elbows and back immediately began to ache in protest, and he tried to put such selfish thoughts aside as he turned his attention to the team.

Tom noticed how physically close Rose was to Carl, such was the intensity of their exchange, and he felt his stomach involuntarily tighten. His mind immediately went to the worst possible reasons, and he had visions of Rose handing in her notice to join Carl at Cornell.

That was the last thing he needed. Good radio astronomers were hard to come by, and Sherrie would be devastated if her best friend left. Tom felt a pang of bitterness and envy rise up inside of him – how could Rose be so thoughtless... all the training he had given her, and now here she was conspiring... conspiring with the enemy.

Their waiting van was surrounded by a police escort that would cut a path for them through the notorious Lorain rush-hour traffic, and as they got in Tom's dismay deepened when his wife sat on the other side of Carl, joining in the discussion with him and Rose. The three of them seemed to have known one another for a lifetime, such was the ease of their conversation. Professor Jenkins felt fear and jealousy course through his system like an army of advancing ants.

Not Sherrie...

He had always been the jealous type. He knew that it was not attractive, and he tried to keep it on a short leash, but *dammit* Sherrie belonged to him. She had no business sitting alongside this stranger and being so familiar with him.

Reid slid in next to him and turned to address the other three. As the van's engine started, he began the next stage of his briefing.

"Ok people, we have maybe a half-hour drive. The source of the signal has been narrowed to within a few square kilometers on this side of Lake Erie. We think that this thing is in an area of forest known as Quarry Creek and..."

Tom shook his head. "I know those woods. I played there as a child... they're not big, maybe twenty square kilometers. If there is anything there then it's new."

Reid nodded and made a note. "Thank you Sir. We're fortunate that the area is not heavily populated. However, as a precaution, we've closed Route Six and Interstate Two..."

Sherrie looked bewildered. "They're the busiest routes. I should know, I've sat on them for just about every Thanksgiving."

Reid held up a hand. "They are just closed between the Quarry Creek junctions, and there're diversions in place. We've staged a train derailing on the nearby freight line and told the locals it's a chemical spill. You'll see lots of hazmat suits about, but don't worry – that's just for show. Now as you can see here..."

Reid opened up a map and began to point to the forest around Quarry Creek. Tom was too familiar with the area and began to drift in his own thoughts.

He had not been back since his father had died eight years ago, and it felt strange to return. Lorain had always been good to him and deep down he felt he had never repaid that debt. His schooling had been first rate, allowing him the career that was the envy of The Barnies, and he had grown up in a stable and safe home. A boy could not ask for more, and yet he knew that he had done nothing in return. At any given opportunity, Tom had played by the rules, giving no ground to those that deserved a break.

The Lieutenant Colonel knew that he could have protected his older brother. The hippy student that Joel had beaten was a draft-dodger at a time when a lot of his friends were in Vietnam, but Tom made no mention of the provocation Joel had endured, knowing how it would look, and no rising star could endure an allegation of a cover-up.

Similarly with Dean Ballantine, Tom could have made mention in his report of the sterling work carried out at the Perkins Observatory and ensured that the team received some kind of recognition. Instead, he had just reported the facts.

Ohio always remembered its debts… and once it had tried to collect. Tom had never forgotten that day – it had been the summer of sixty-eight… not long before Old Man Jenkins had passed away. Tom knew that his father was ill – he could hear by the rattling of his breathing that The Cancer was eating away at his lungs, and they - including Rose who had become like family - had gone for a daytrip to the beach.

Rose had not long returned from a holiday in Egypt and she and Sherrie had gossiped all day about the amazing temples she had seen. Later in the afternoon, the two women had bought a half-hour on one of the speedboats that always offered such rides at that time of year, and Tom had stayed on the sandy shore with his father, listening to their shrieks and whoops.

And then the damn-fool of a pilot had pushed it too far. The speedboat crested a wave, its hull completely emerging from the water, and when it slammed down both Sherrie and Rose had been thrown into the dark waters of Lake Erie.

Tom was on his feet in seconds, sprinting into the small waves that lapped hungrily at the shoreline. He knew that they were too far out for him to reach, but that had not stopped him.

Panic had swept over him as his mind tried to conceive the intensity of grief he would be subjected to if his wife drowned… the gaping void in his life that Sherrie would leave if she… she made him who he was, and he dreaded the thing he would become without her constant presence.

They were fine. They bobbed to the surface, their life-jackets inflated and they were completely unharmed.

Nevertheless, those few seconds had felt like a lifetime, and that day Tom had realized an awful truth: *Ohio never forgets what it's owed.*

"… and have there been any previous indications of something in the vicinity?" Carl was asking, pointing at the area on the map where Quarry Creek met Lake Erie.

"Nothing tangible," Reid replied. "Every town has its stories, but…"

"Lorain has plenty of those," Tom interrupted, remembering the urban legends of his youth. "There were any number of Iroquoian tribes living here before colonization. They told the pilgrims of a creature in the lake but it was just a tale, although for a while the State University thought it might be some kind of surviving prehistoric squid or octopus. Then there were more recent stories. Various generations of settlers wrote accounts of lights in the sky, followed by the arrival of strangers who brought with them wealth and madness. From the descriptions, it was probably just some sort of borealis and a simpleton being conned."

"What about that one you told me?" Sherrie asked. "That story, about those people who disappeared?"

Tom started, scarcely believing that he had forgotten the story that had haunted his youth. "God yes… I forgot that one. It was fifty years before I was born, but my old man used to tell me this story his father told him. Part of it was true, but the rest of it? I imagine it was just kids trying to scare each other. In 1873… this was before the town was called Lorain. Back then it was 'The Mouth of The Black River'. Anyway, there was this little district on the western outskirts - some sort of textile hub or something - and the people there were doing well. Then one day, they were gone. Dinner left on the table, washing on the line, but three hundred people were just gone.

"The sheriff at the time investigated but there was no trace of them. The Mayor signed their death certificates in a hurry and then claimed their homes as Council property before selling them and pocketing the proceeds himself. The next year the town was renamed Lorain."

"That sounds pretty suspect," Reid said. "Does anyone know what really happened?"

Tom shook his head. "Not for sure. It's no secret that those people had difficulties with the mayor – something about contaminated crops and bad seeds. Some think that the mayor sent the sheriff and a posse in to clear the troublesome families and it got out of hand. Others say that they probably just moved to get away from the mayor. Of course, when I was a kid there were all sorts of stories going around; ghosts and ghouls and demons – the usual fare. But like you said Agent, every town has its stories."

The occupants of the speeding van fell silent, each lost in their own thoughts as they compared what Tom had told them to their mission brief, and then wrote it off as the imaginings of a lesser informed people.

Tom looked out of the window at the blur that was his hometown, as their convoy cut a swathe through the near stationary traffic that was struggling to deal with the diversion Reid's men had put in place. Professor Jenkins had not been back in such a long time… but the whole city looked old and worn by the freezing grip of winter. Some shops were boarded up, and in a few places he could see where plaster had cracked and water had seeped in.

He was not surprised. The town was close enough to Cleveland to see all its investment sucked away. Younger families did not want to live here because of the long commute and the retirees could afford to go to Miami where the cold did not seep into their bones the way it did here.

27

That left Lorain with a dwindling population and fewer tax revenues to carry out more maintenance. Tom doubted the town would last another twenty years. Sure, the new Ford assembly line might count for something, but it was just a stop gap – there were plenty of states who would tout for a business that size, with lower taxes and other incentives.

As they passed Providence Bar, Sherrie caught Tom's wistful glance and saw him rub his right forearm absently. His tattoo was one of the few things from his past that he would talk about, and the design was of an entwined knuckle duster over crossed revolvers, and a cut throat razor leading into swallows holding a scroll linked to a set of boxing gloves. She knew that he shared it with his best friend – Adam Cannon – and it was a memento both of their teenage boxing days and the trouble the two boys had caused in their halcyon youth. Sherrie knew better than to interrupt Tom when he was reminiscing with himself.

Tom smiled as he remembered Providence Bar. Adam's father had owned it from the turn of the century and it had been in the family until the bank foreclosed on it in the early seventies. The ghosts of his indiscretions stood out on the sidewalk, eyeing him in wonder.

The time when he and a fourteen year old Adam had snuck out half-empty liquor bottles when his father was in the basement changing a barrel...

Throwing up into the gutter on his eighteenth birthday...

The two nineteen year olds running hell for leather to the sanctuary of its paneled walls at two in the morning... their friend, Jason, just a few yards behind.

What did you do? What the f...

I didn't do nothing... she just fell over...

She's just an Injun... let The Barnies take the rap.

The ghost solidified and their voices echoed inside his skull as the shadows lengthened, bringing that fateful night back.

A young Adam, flushed with the first testosterone-fuelled glow of manhood, pointed at Jason in the darkened bar, his breath reeking of cheap beer and violence. "This is your fault. You shouldda left her alone."

"I swear... I just wanted to see what she was doing," the slighter boy protested, staggering as his system tried to cope with the unaccustomed belly full of alcohol.

Adam did not let it go. "You'd no business... it's one of their... their rituals or something."

"My daddy says it's heathen," Tom interjected, trying to focus through the vapors of liquor. "What them Injuns do up there..."

Jason looked from Tom back to Adam. "You see. Tom agrees. She was doing black magic or voodoo..."

"I don't believe that and nor do you... she was just...."

"What?" Jason barked. "You saw what she was doing. She was all naked with her titties out and grinding herself against a tree..."

Adam stepping up to Jason, staring him down. "She was just getting off... that's their way. You didn't need to go up to her..."

Whilst Adam was his best friend, Tom did not agree. "It was something else Adam. C'mon... there were animals and stuff looking at her. All those ravens and that deer... man that was something else. I ain't saying what Jase did was right... but dammit, that *was* some black magic."

"I swear," Jason protested. "I didn't touch her. She just..."

Adam was in no mood for excuses. "What? The Injun girl wouldn't give it up to you and... what she just fell over and hit her head on a rock and bashed her brains out?"

Jason looked to the floor and began to mumble. "I just wanted to see if... if she wanted some fun, you know."

Adam took hold of his one time friend by the shoulders, his facing contorting into a snarl. "You ain't got no business... they're savages. You know that. You might as well rut with a Barnie." He turned to address Tom but found him absent. "Where's he gone?"

"I'm right here," a voice came from the back bar, and Tom emerged, carrying a jerry can of kerosene.

"What's that for?" Adam asked.

"What do you think?" Tom spat. "You two grab the shovels. We'll go back up there and finish this right. Ain't nobody going to jail over some heathen slut..."

Providence Bar sped past and as their convoy made its way into the western districts, Tom tried to put that night from his mind. As they sped through what passed for downtown, the ghosts began to fade, until they passed the spot where the three young men had turned onto a rough track that led up to the woods where they would dig a pit and...

The memory broke as Tom saw unfamiliar shops in buildings he recognized. The march of progress was relentless. As they got deeper into the residential district, he could see that the front yards were becoming increasingly unkempt and the grass grew longer the further out they travelled. Although the winter had done its best to beat it into a necrotic brown, he could make out the tendrils of what looked like bindweed as it tried to push under wooden slats and moldering mortar.

Gershom's voice came back to him. *It's an invasive species Sir. It's everywhere... all around you. You could walk by and never even know it was there.*

"This is it," Reid said, as the van pulled off the empty highway and onto a small track that led up to a forest.

"It seems so strange," Sherrie said to Tom as they exited the van. "I've only ever known this road to be filled with traffic," she nodded to the highway they had just left, and pulled on a thick jacket to stave off the cold

Tom grunted an acknowledgement.

"Hun? You ok?" Sherrie asked, touching his arm.

Tom looked across the road to the shoreline of Lake Erie, and tried to avoid telling what his wife what he was really thinking about. "Uh-huh. Just remembering the last time we were on that beach."

Sherrie smiled. "It was years ago and we were fine."

The forest wore a light covering of snow like a thin coat, similar to those The Barnies clothed themselves with in such weather, to prove to the white collar families how they could tough it outside whilst their softer contemporaries shivered next to the fire.

The smell of pine and oak filled Tom's nose, and for a brief moment he felt homesick for this place as he remembered childhood games on the beach and in the forest. Saying nothing, he nodded towards the two approaching figures in bright orange hazmat suits.

"That'll be the welcoming committee," Rose said, joining them.

"Make sure they take care with the equipment," Tom replied. "Some of that stuff is sensitive."

Reid was walking over to greet the hazmats, and Tom joined him, pulling on his own regulation jacket as he did so. Men had been known to freeze to death out here in midwinter.

"I'm Agent Reid. You should have been informed that I was coming."

"We have sir," the first said, removing her helmet to reveal a pale woman in her mid thirties with a shock of dark hair. "I'm Doctor Bahnsen, this is Special Agent Dales. The coroner is just finishing up, and he'll be down in minute or so."

Tom and Reid looked to each other in confusion. "Coroner?" Tom asked.

Dr Bahnsen held up a transparent bag and Tom thought he was going to faint. It was not that the bag contained a severed human arm that filled his mouth with the bitter taste of imminent bile; it was the tattoo that was exactly like his.

An entwined knuckle duster over two crossed revolvers, and a cut throat razor leading into swallows holding a scroll linked to a set of boxing gloves.

There was only one man in the world, other than Lieutenant-Colonel Jenkins, who had that tattoo. Adam Cannon.

As soon as America had entered The War, Tom enlisted, both in a bid to leave the corrosive memories of his hometown behind him, and to atone for his actions through National Service. When he had returned briefly in the late forties, he found Adam running the boxing club by day and working behind his father's bar by night. They had talked a little, but the distance that had come between them nearly ten years ago was now an unbridgeable chasm.

"Are there any more up there?" Reid asked, looking up the forest trail.

Bahnsen shook her head. "We don't think so... but he's spread out everywhere. Something got hold of him... like a bear or something."

"Have you indentified the body?" Reid pressed.

Tom coughed, trying to choke down the cud that had been festering at the back of his throat every since he had seen the arm. "I... I think it's a local man. I knew someone in my youth who had that tattoo. They used to own the bar in town... I'm not sure where they are now, but ask the Sheriff for the Cannons' address. He'll have it."

Reid looked to Tom in concern. "Sir? Are you well? You've gone quite pale." He looked over Tom's shoulder and motioned to Sherrie to come up.

"I'm fine," Tom replied quickly, holding out a hand that told Sherrie to stay where she was.

"Sir, I understand if you knew the victim... if you're not able to carry on..." Reid continued.

Tom glared at him. *You'd just love that, wouldn't you?* "I told you, I'm fine," he replied and then turned to the two agents. "Who else knows about this?"

"It's contained Sir. The coroner is from the local field office."

"Great," Tom said a little too sharply. "Have you identified the source of the signal?"

"Yes Sir," Bahnsen replied. "There's some sort of cave network about half a mile up. This body..." she held up the bag. "Was found just outside. We were told not to enter until you arrived... but even at the entrance..." Bahnsen's voice faded as she struggled for the words.

"What is it Doctor?" Reid asked.

"Well Sir... outside of the cave mouth our instruments work fine... but when we get up to the entrance... everything scrambles."

"What do you mean, everything?" Tom queried.

"None of our electronics work... and they don't come back on when we move away. It's as if the circuits have been fried."

Reid turned to Tom. "Sir, can your equipment handle this?"

"I don't know Agent... unlikely. The doctor is describing some sort of electro-magnetic field. Maybe some sort of lead-lined housing might offer protection, but we only carry a little. If the effect is as severe as the doctor says, we'd need to get more from DC."

"Uh, Sirs?" Bahnsen said cautiously. "There is something else you should be aware of..."

"What's that, Doctor?" Reid replied.

"Ummm..." Bahnsen pointed towards the sky and Tom and Reid followed the line of her finger.

A single contrail could be seen, widening across the clear cold cerulean sky.

"Agent?" Tom asked. "I would imagine that the FAA would have been instructed to declare this area a no-fly zone."

"Yes Sir, they were."

"Then what are we looking at?"

"Uh Sirs?" Bahnsen said again. "We've already informed Division. Section Twenty-Three arrived thirty minutes ago."

Tom knew Section Twenty-Three only too well. These were the spooks that made even the likes of Agent Reid nervous. Highly trained killing machines, it was said that no Section Twenty-Three agent had ever died during an operation, nor had one ever failed to complete their mission. They were the best of the best, and it was rumored that only one out of every ten thousand applicants was successful.

Reid's voice was strained. "How many of them are there?"

"I don't know Sir. Maybe forty or so," Bahnsen replied. "Their commanding officer – Captain Graves – is up at the cave mouth."

Reid looked nervously to Tom and then back to Bahnsen. "Has there been any ground activity? Has anyone tried to breach the perimeter?"

Bahnsen shook her head. "Not that I know of Sir."

"Thank you Doctor," Reid said. "We'll call if we need you."

Tom turned quickly on his heel and made his way back to the van.

"What's the hurry Sir?" Reid asked.

Tom looked back at the younger man and frowned, unsure whether he was being serious. When he saw that he was, he answered. "We may have the lead on the Soviets for the time being, but tell me this, Agent, do you really want to be here if there is a firefight between Section Twenty-Three and The Spets?"

He did not wait for an answer but addressed his team as soon as he arrived back at the van. "Ok... it looks like we have a live arena. Rose; grab the geiger counters. Sherrie; the dosimeters. Apparently there is a cave up on the rise that is putting something out that is frying all electronics. Carl; there is some lead lining in the back – it's not much but it should be enough to jerry-rig into one of the smaller two-way radio units. If you can protect the circuits we should be able to use it if... if we meet anything down there."

Rose and Carl began to get the equipment out, but Sherrie stayed where she was. "What's the cave putting out Tom?"

"I've no idea. It sounds like some EM field. Why do you ask?"

"Didn't you say in the van that this whole area had a reputation for lights in the sky followed by the arrival of strangers?"

"Yes. So?"

"Tom... think about the Northern Lights. A borealis is just charged particles striking the atmosphere. It's a super massive EM field."

Tom frowned, not following his wife's train of thought. "You think the cave is sucking up charged particles? I've never heard..."

Sherrie tried not to roll her eyes at her husband's blinkeredness. "No hun… what if the stories of this place are true? What if the cave is the *cause* of the lights and…"

Reid finished the sentence for her. "… then we might be expecting strangers."

Tom wanted to scoff. The idea of extra-terrestrials living in a cave in Ohio was ridiculous. And yet he did not laugh. Whilst there was something fantastical at work here, it felt as though Lorain was finally revealing its secret self to him and, if he was right, he would have an opportunity to put his hometown on the map.

And that would repay all of his debts.

"Come on," he said gruffly. "Let's get up to this cave."

CHAPTER 3

Through the night and the wind and the rain,
And the harvest of the flood,
I can feel Her calling,
A debt to be paid with my blood.

"The Call of The Black River" by Even The Lost.
© G & L Tate 1978

Captain Graves was a large man who, when he spoke, sounded like a whispering mountain. Tom supposed that when you measured seven feet in every direction, it was not necessary to shout.

The briefing was succinct and to the point; Section Twenty-Three had secured the forest and had ventured into the cave entrance. However, when their communication equipment had failed, Graves had pulled them out and waited for Agent Reid and his team, choosing to have his men move the various equipment crates from their vehicles up to the cave entrance where they now formed a neat semi-circle.

The evidence of a dry autumn giving way to a cold winter was all about them, with crisp brown leaves lining the forest floor, not yet having begun their slow submission to decay. Small mounds of snow lay clumped on the ground, like miniature sentinels to a hidden underground world, and Tom could not help but marvel at the beauty and inevitability of Nature, as She reminded all who would listen that every living thing must return to soil.

Despite the allure of the wild landscape about them, Tom's team listened to the briefing in near silence. The air was heavy like that of an abattoir, and although no-one said anything, Tom knew that the cold touch of death had taken his one-time friend's hand only a few hours earlier.

He tried to put the notion of what might have happened to Adam from his mind as he approached Captain Graves. "Captain?"

"Yessir?" the larger man said, turning smartly to face a superior officer. At this proximity Tom appreciated the sheer size of the man. A barrel chest supported equally muscular, although unadorned, arms and he reminded Tom of his days at the boxing club.

"I believe that we know each other, but I am having difficulty placing…"

"Yessir. We met in fifty-two. Of course I was just a Second-Lieutenant then."

"Fifty-two?" Tom pondered more to himself than to the Captain. "You were at Groom Lake?"

Captain Graves nodded smartly. "Yessir. You were on the panel that discovered those tunnels after that nuke had been tested. I led the team after taking a briefing from yourself."

"Oh course, the abandoned silver mines…"

"Long abandoned, Sir. They went down and back further than I've ever known. Dangerously unstable, Sir. We were lucky to only lose one man when the tunnel began to collapse."

"And you're a captain now I see."

"Yessir. You know what they say; life advances when you pay your debts."

Tom frowned, not recognizing the phrase, and at that moment Agent Reid approached. "Lieutenant Colonel, if I may?"

The Captain nodded curtly as Reid dismissed him and turned to Tom. "How do you want to play this?"

Tom smiled to himself. Despite being the nominal leader of the operation, the boy knew he was out of his depth and was now deferring with increasing regularity to Tom's experienced head. Grey hairs were starting to count for something – perhaps this really would be good for him.

He reasoned through his options and then looked to Sherrie and Rose. "Are the counters picking anything up?"

They both shook their heads. "I've got nothing," Rose answered.

"Very well. Rose, take a geiger and a dosimeter and go up to the entrance – see if you can get a reading."

As they watched the svelte form of the younger woman approach the cave, Reid murmured to him. "Sir, do we really have time for this?"

"I want to get in there as much as you do Agent," Tom muttered in reply. "But there is no point in rushing in if we're not going to come out again."

"It's gone out," Rose called back to them, waving the Geiger counter at them. She was only a few yards into the cave and the late morning sun was reflecting off the red hematite rock. For a moment it seemed that she was wearing a mask of blood, and Tom's breath caught in his chest.

The moment passed as she made her way back down to them. "Did the dosimeter pick anything up?" Carl asked, his voice heavy with worry.

Tom found himself frowning again. Carl had only been with them for a few hours and now he was acting as though they were all his closest friends. Tom decided that his concern was feigned, and that the man was probably just currying favor.

"No, nothing at all," Rose replied, looking at her dosimeter counter.

"Carl," Tom said without emotion, "take that little two-way up there. See if the lead lining holds up."

They watched him move up to the cave mouth and turn the radio on. There had been just enough lead left over to provide cover for a couple of torches. Despite Carl's efforts to ingratiate himself, Tom found himself hoping for him to meet a wholly alien end.

"It's working," Carl called back down.

"Ok, go a little further in and see if it holds out." Tom shouted back.

"Uh, Tom…" Rose began, holding up the innards of her Geiger counter as she sought to determine the source of the equipment failure.

"What have you got?" he replied, Sherrie joining him at her friend's side.

"It's like Doctor Bahnsen said – it's just been knocked out."

"Let me see," Sherrie responded, taking holding of the wires. "She's right Tom. It's been fried. The solder on the circuits has been melted…"

Reid interrupted them. "Is there any risk to health?"

Sherrie and Rose looked at each other and shrugged in unison. Sherrie answered for them. "Difficult to say – it's electro-magnetic radiation, but I'll be damned if I recognize it," Sherrie said. "If it's ionizing then it could easily be lethal within a matter of minutes, depending on the amplitude. But…"

Reid looked to Tom. "You just sent Doctor Sagan in there…"

Tom was already running up the gentle slope to the cave mouth, dead leaves crunching underfoot like shattering skeletons. "Carl. Carl! Where are…"

"Yes?" the charismatic doctor replied, materializing out the gloom.

"Are you ok?"

"Yes."

"Headache?"

"No, what is…?"

"Step outside. Let me look at you," Tom ordered, as Sherrie, Rose and Reid joined him.

Carl walked forward and squinted into the wintery sunlight. "What's going on?" he asked.

"Sherrie thought that the radiation might be ionizing and…" Reid began.

"No, I didn't," Sherrie interrupted. "I said *if*. You men never listen."

Rose stifled a snigger and Professor Jenkins glared at his wife, letting her know in no uncertain terms that she was crossing a line by ridiculing him and Reid so publicly.

"I don't think so," Carl said cheerily, waving his two-way at them. "I'm getting nothing. Ionizing radiation would have a radio component to its decay... I'm getting nothing but background."

Tom frowned again. "Nothing at all?"

"No, why?"

"I would have expected something," Tom began. "Maybe some sort of residue. If something is transmitting from this cave, then at least some of the signal would bounce around."

"It only broadcasts every twenty-three hours," Reid replied. "It's not due until twenty-two-hundred tonight."

"Tom's right," Carl said. "There should be something, even if it's just an echo. What's the frequency of the signal?"

Reid flicked through a beige folder. "Let's see... ummm, you guys probably understand this better than I do... here it is. One hundred and sixty gigahertz... What?"

The teams' expression had collectively fallen.

"What?" Reid asked again. "What is it?"

"Let me see that," Tom said, snatching the folder from the agent.

The three other scientists crowded around him, looking over his shoulder into the file.

Sherrie looked up. "This wasn't in our individual briefings. Why weren't we told about this?"

Reid shook his head, not understanding the significance. "Central office marked it as strictly need to know... and no-one asked until now. Why? What is it?"

Tom raised his head from the file and looked critically at the agent. "You know what the Big Bang Theory is?"

"The beginning of the universe... expansion, right?"

"And you understand that every sound has its own frequency?"

"Yes Sir, I do." Reid was getting sick of Tom's condescension.

"One hundred and sixty gigahertz is the frequency of the Big Bang... it's the sound of the universe."

"Tom," Rose said, looking up. "I don't like this."

"She's right," Sherrie agreed. "This is something else... extra-terrestrial maybe, but this could be a whole other level of technology. We should get a bigger team... I don't know if we're qualified for this."

Tom looked to Reid and then to his wife. "We don't have the time."

The agent still did not understand. "What does the frequency mean? What does it change?"

"You understand what a sound wave is?" Tom said, losing patience. "Going from Point A to B?"

Reid nodded. "Yes Sir, I do."

"Well it takes time. If a radio signal left Earth it would take thousands of years to get to even the nearest star."

"Yes Sir, I understand…"

"I very much doubt that," Tom interrupted. "The further your signal needs to go the more power it needs because the more resistance it encounters. Except if you broadcast at one hundred and sixty gigahertz… it would take next to no time at all to reach its destination, because you are using the universe as your own personal amplifier. Do you understand? The cosmos becomes a giant transducer… broadcasting to itself from all points simultaneously. But the technology required to broadcast at that frequency… just the amount of power that would be required… Sherrie's right. We're out of our depth. We're talking experimental physics here… quantum particles – it's Einstein-level thinking. We've no idea how long this… this thing has been broadcasting for. Whatever it's calling to may have been and gone already, or may arrive just as we get in there.

"But understand this, Agent… to have the technological capability… it's far beyond anything we could manage. It rules out that a human could have built this. What worries me is if someone's started operating whatever transmitter is down there with no understanding of what they're actually doing. They may be trying to crack into that power source and… well, if it blew a fuse you wouldn't want to be around. Worse still, if they've adapted the energy source into a weapon…we're going to need troops. And I mean the elite variety."

Reid's walkie-talkie squawked with the voice of Captain Graves. "Go ahead," the agent replied.

"We've visual on a second Soviet plane."

"How high Captain?" Reid asked.

"Same as before. Fifty thousand. Either they're trying to provoke us, or they're keeping an eye on their own assets."

Tom nodded to him. "Ask him for his assessment."

"Did you hear that Captain?"

"I did. We're preparing for incoming."

Tom looked to Sherrie and then back to Reid. "If we get caught out here we'll be sitting ducks."

"I'm authorized to issue you with sidearms only. But Sir, I need you to call a go-no-go on the cave."

Tom and Sherrie exchanged glances with Rose – the presence of the Soviets changed everything. "In my opinion," Tom began, "there is almost certainly extra-terrestrial technology in there, although who or what is operating it is unknown, as is their purpose. Given the Russians' interest…

and that their investigation appears to be more advanced than our own, I'd recommend entry. Certainly there do not appear to be any ill effects from whatever is knocking out our equipment but I would recommend proceeding with caution. It's a go."

"Very good Sir," Reid said, and opened a nearby supply crate and began handing out Beretta hand guns. "Dr Jenkins... Dr Santiago... do you ladies know how to use these?"

Sherrie and Rose nodded, and took the pistols by their black grips, holstering them expertly.

"Dr Sagan?"

Carl shook his head and held his hands up, refusing the gun. "No... I never learned..."

Typical, Tom thought. *Another draft dodger.*

"Very well Doctor," Reid replied...

The report of a rifle echoed through the forest and Reid's radio burst into life. *"Contact! I have contact!"*

Tom and Reid instantly dropped to the ground, pulling their weapons as they did so.

"Get down," Tom hissed to Sherrie, Rose and Carl, pulling his wife down by her sleeve.

The radio crackled again. *"Incoming, incoming... contact!"*

More gunfire reverberated through the trees and Tom had the creeping feeling that Section Twenty-Three were about to lose their coveted status of never having lost a man.

"Reid!" That was Graves' voice on the radio.

"Reid here. Copy."

"Multiple hostiles inbound. Get Professor Jenkins into..."

The sound of rifle reports came from all about them, and Tom could hear soldiers crashing through the forest, no more than two hundred yards from their position.

"Acknowledged," Reid said into his radio, unsure whether the captain was still alive.

Tom looked first to his wife and then to Reid. "We need to get into that cave."

*

The red hematite rock quickly gave way to the impassive grey of granite, and whilst the cave tunnel bucked and twisted like a giant worm frozen in a death throe, the ceiling remained high enough that they could all stand.

Tom and Reid had taken the two torches that Carl had prepared and led the party cautiously into the pitch dark. The sound of the firefight in the forest quickly faded as they made their way deeper and it was not long before a moldering damp smell greeted them.

"Are these tunnels safe?" Carl asked, worried that such wet rock might collapse at any time.

Tom and Reid answered in unison. "Probably." The two men frowned at each other as they jockeyed for leadership, and continued edging forward.

"The air is not stale. It could be water from a stream..." Tom ventured. "It's probably one of the tributaries that feeds The Black River, or maybe even The Creek. Either way, it's unlikely to penetrate the earth too much."

As he finished, the tunnel abruptly widened into a deep cavern, and the party stopped to take in this wondrous feat of nature.

The width of the cavern was such that the beams from their respective torches did not reach the sides, but the rough ceiling had come low, giving the entirety the impression of being a cyclopean ellipse. The floor slipped gently away from them, sloping down at a shallow angle as if slowly spiraling down into the heart of the Earth.

Reid's voice was filled with awe. "How far back do you think it goes?"

Tom shook his head, forgetting that he could not be seen in the dark. "I have no idea. Carl," he turned, pointing his torch beam to where Doctor Sagan stood. "Have you got anything on that radio?"

Carl flicked a few buttons. "Nothing."

"Are you sure it's working?" pressed Tom.

"It's got power, which is more than the other units had."

"Tom," came the disembodied voice of Sherrie. "Can you swing your torch over here... on my dosimeter"

Professor Jenkins shone his torch at his wife's hip. "What is it?"

"I just wanted to see if we have any readings," she replied.

"And?"

There was a moment's pause. "No, nothing."

"What should we do?" Rose asked, gazing at the subterranean vista before them. "This is too big for just us to explore..."

Reid turned to Tom. "It's your call Sir. You need to make the threat assessment."

Tom considered the options. "Well, I don't fancy our chances topside. We don't know who our men were engaging or how many there are... but I'd bet they aren't Canadians."

Despite the tensions, the others chuckled to themselves.

"Bottom line is we're here, and there's no immediate risk. We'll press on... but if this cavern... whatever it is... if it looks to be unstable, well then we'll reassess. Let's go."

"Ah, Professor Jenkins?" That was Carl.

"Yes?"

"Um... you said you played around here as a child? Well... have you ever heard of this place?"

Tom cast his eyes to the floor momentarily, trying to forget that the Indian girl was not buried too far from where they stood, and then looked back to Doctor Sagan. "No. Let's keep moving."

The party moved forward into the darkness, their footsteps echoing like the gunshots they had left behind. Despite his cool exterior, Tom bristled at the impertinence of Sagan's question… but also knew what it meant.

He had played in the woods above throughout his childhood, and he knew that there was not a boy in his circle of friends who would not have ventured into this place had they found it. Yet, with the exception of the disappearances in 1873, Lorain had a relatively uninteresting public profile. There was always the occasional drunkard, or sometimes a kid would get caught shoplifting, but there was seldom a murder much less a missing child… and Tom knew that a place like this would have sucked them in.

The Indian girl's disappearance had not even made the local paper, and there were times that Tom wondered if he had dreamt the whole thing.

As they ventured deeper into the gloom, he occasionally cast his torchlight up to the ceiling, noting the myriad of roots and fleshy tendrils that protruded. He thought about what Gershom had said.

It's everywhere… all around you. You could walk by and never even know it was there.

"What's that?" Rose's voice came high and quick.

"What?" Reid replied.

"Over to the left… where your torch just was."

The beam played slowly back.

"There," Rose said, confirming the spot.

A pyramid of rock rose up from the dank earth.

"It's a stalagmite," Reid said. "It's formed from water dripping through calcium carbonate bearing rocks from above. Look," he pointed to the rough ceiling. "See that raised area there? That's a stalactite. That's where it's dripping from. In a few thousand years, they'll probably merge together."

"There's another one over there," Sherrie said. Fifty yards ahead was another impressive cone rising from the ground, a little larger than the first.

They slowly followed the line of the stalagmites and, as they did, the atmosphere between them became increasingly tense. It was not just that these pinnacles of rock were coming at *exactly* fifty yards, it was the shape that they were taking on. The further they went, the more regular in form they became, until they were perfectly worked columns supporting the ceiling above.

As they approached another colonnade, Tom stopped, letting his torchlight play over what was now plainly the effort of many hands.

He turned to Reid. "Are you seeing this?"

The younger man nodded. "I thought I saw it on a few back there… but I wasn't sure. What do you make of it?"

Tom shook his head as his torch picked out well etched pictograms that wound around the column. What they said or meant was completely beyond him and yet he felt something rising up from deep within to tug at his conscious self, calling out.

"Damned if I know," he finally replied. "I've heard about cave paintings in Europe and down in South America... but here?"

"I think these are more than cave paintings," Rose replied. "Do you remember that trip I took to Egypt? A lot of temples out there had columns with carvings on them."

Reid had turned back to Tom. "Is that what this is? Could this be a temple?"

Professor Jenkins felt four pairs of eyes fall upon him expectantly. "I... I have no idea."

"What about that?" Reid turned his light to the ceiling, and Tom saw a thick tendril, like those he had seen back in Washington, and then later on their drive through Lorain, working its way down. Yet unlike its predecessors, this did not bore into the rock of the column, but rather wound its way around a purpose built groove that spiraled from top to bottom.

"I saw them earlier on," Tom confessed, "but I have no idea what..."

He broke off as his gaze followed the ringlets of vine down the column. It seemed impossible, yet at the base it appeared to merge with the stone. Tom cautiously reached out, feeling its rocky skin and then a few inches higher where it reverted to soft flesh. He had no explanation other than maybe the stem was sucking up the still wet carbonate from the cavern floor.

He was so absorbed with trying to understand the relationship between the column and the Creeping Crowsfoot, that he only caught the end of Sherrie's whisper.

"... *doesn't remember.*"

"What was that, hun?" he said swinging his beam around.

"Nothing. I was just asking Rose if she saw any plants around the columns in Egypt."

Tom trained the torch on Rose. "Did you?"

Doctor Santiago shook her head. "No. Beyond the irrigation ditches of the Nile, it's too dry for anything to grow."

Tom stood, casting his torchlight out into the seemingly eternal darkness, and tried to comprehend the power of an alien artifact that could transmit through all the rock that surrounded them. He turned, looking back at the way they had all come, weighing the possible threat of what lay behind them and what was ahead. And then there was Proxmire. If he could find something down here, it would permanently derail the senator's investigation and guarantee his department's funding.

"Sir?" Reid asked. "Do you think we should go back?"

"I'm not sure. We're a long way down... but let's press on."

As they moved forward, the smell of damp earth increased, and Tom guessed that whatever underground tributary he had previously theorized was close at hand. Privately, he felt claustrophobic in this cavern, and he hoped that the subterranean river would be substantial enough to impede any further progress.

He was not to be disappointed.

They had walked for another fifteen minutes when they came to the edge of a vast pool. The length extended fully from one wall to the other, and the water was clear, stretching down until the light of the torches was swallowed by the inky depths of the lagoon.

The pool was not as wide as its length, and on the opposite bank Tom could see a faint purple phosphorescence that suggested that whatever was responsible for the radio signal was close at hand. He could not help but notice that the stems that wound their way around the earlier columns were thicker here, streaming along the cavern roof, either towards or away from the source of the unearthly glow ahead.

Yet, despite their goal being within sight, Tom could see no way across the pool and, with the possibility of contamination from whatever was before them, he resolved that this was as far as this journey would take them.

As he turned to address the others, something flitted at the corner of his vision, and he snapped back, his eyes straining in the gloom to the source of the glow on the opposite bank. Something was moving back there… something was sliding in some sort of viscous liquid that slurped nosily like a swarm of eels flopping on the wet floor.

Against the glimmering of whatever was at the back of the cave, Tom saw a shape begin to take form and his breath caught in his chest. He knew it. As sure as he knew that Reid had deliberately led him down here with his chivvying and chiding, Tom Jenkins knew the muscular silhouette of his best friend that was now emerging from the shadows on the opposite bank, and the form of Adam Cannon began to solidify before him.

To his shock, Reid entered the water and began to wade across.

"Agent!" he cried out. "Stop! What are you…"

Reid turned, and with a snap of his arm reached out to take Professor Jenkins' wrist. "Come now Tom," he said, all respect for the man's station evaporating from his voice. "You must be purified before you can meet The Outer Dreamer."

Tom struggled against the younger man who seemed possessed of a strength beyond that possible for a mere human. Feeling his feet sinking into the silty bottom, Tom reached to his hip with his free hand and brought his pistol to bear, discharging it as he did so into Reid's chest.

The report echoed around the chamber, like the dying cry of a prehistoric beast.

The Agent recoiled but did not let go. "Ow," he mocked, looking down at the dark viscous fluid that pumped from his wound, and began to pull Tom deeper into the pool.

Rose came from behind, laying a reassuring hand on Tom's shoulder and, taking his elbow with the other, began pushing him under the surface.

"Come now Tom," she said reassuringly. "All debts must be paid. This will be good for you."

As he slipped into the now roiling depths, Tom's mind snapped back to 1944.

*

The wave of water that crashed into the shattered cockpit of Kismet's Reach slapped Tom from his daze.

The mangled frame of the once mighty bomber plunged down into the vastness of the ocean, and he struggled to release the webbing that secured him to his seat.

Captain Gustafsson's body floated gently upwards, free of its restraints, and a knowing smile seemed to play upon the older man's lips, as though there was an irony in such an end.

Tom tried to hold his breath as he fought to release himself from his chair, and he felt his lungs begin to burn as the light from the surface faded from view. Kismet's Reach bored down into a cold darkness so complete that Tom shivered as a conviction arose that not even God himself could see the youngest Jenkins boy in the eternal night of the deep ocean.

But something else saw him.

With his lungs on fire, Tom saw a faint purple glow in the murk below him, and something reached out.

It seemed like nothing at first – a faint wisp followed by a few errant bubbles. And then something shifted. Some vast primal bulk moved at the edge of sight, and the wisps became more substantial, solidifying first into thin vine-like tendrils… and then into monstrous muscular tentacles that only the deepest night could have given birth to.

They contracted and then stretched to the fullest extent of his vision, until the black ocean itself had been utterly obliterated, and whatever monstrous leviathan that had been called up from the depths spoke directly into Tom's mind.

Child of The Twilight Ash… know well the voice of your Mother, and the debt you owe. By my word, and my word alone, your time will not yet be at an end. You will know power and pleasures untold if you forever heed my call…

… Heed my call.

… Heed my call.

… Heed myyy calllll.

And there, on the edge of life, young Tom Jenkins made his deal.

*

Sherrie looked on as a swell rose from the deep of the pool. For the briefest of moments, a colossal length of muscle broke free of the water before wrapping around her husband like a lover's embrace, and then returned to the stygian depths.

She recalled that summer's day, not so many years ago, when she and Rose had been catapulted from the safety of their speedboat, and they too had accepted the offer to heed the call of The Great Mother.

Carl stood next to her, his face a mask of horror and wonder, and when her radio squawked the nervous scientist jumped.

"Graves here. Copy?"

"Doctor Jenkins receiving."

"Has he returned?" The radio asked.

"Affirmative."

"Willingly?"

Sherrie considered her husband's final frenzied, and ultimately futile struggles. "Not exactly."

The radio was silent for a moment. "The Outer Dreamer will not be pleased, Sherrie... you know the rules. We have to go willingly or..."

"I know the rules, Captain. But... I don't know what was wrong with him. He'd either forgotten or didn't hear or... I don't know. But it's done now."

"Copy that. We'll clear up out here. Over and out."

Carl's face betrayed the strain he felt inside. "There were never any Russians?"

Sherrie shook her head as the soaking wet forms of Reid and Rose emerged from the water, their faces impassive as if they had no done more than gut a recently caught fish.

"No," she replied. "We had to make Tom want to come here. That's how the deal works; you have to want to do what must be done."

"Like when he married you... and employed Rose? And chose to come here?"

"It only works by freewill," Sherrie confirmed, as her torchlight illuminated the waters at her feet, and the beam picked out some of the three-hundred skeletons of the textile merchants and their families who had come before. "Tom got everything he ever wanted. His father was proud of him for his qualifications. He had a station that commanded respect, a career that was the envy of his peers... and a woman who would do anything for him. You don't want to know how many times The Great Mother had to intervene to keep everything on track... the farmer who rescued him from his crashed bomber; the intervention of Professor Rooksby when he failed his first year of university; Richelle Dawkins... she dated him for such a long time, making him ready to meet me. If he and his friends had not interrupted our servant's rite they would never have come to the attention of The Outer Dreamer, he would never have had a debt to pay... to make it so that you would be his successor."

Carl pretended to understand. "What about him?" he asked, nodding to the still figure on the opposite bank.

Sherrie averted her eyes and took Carl's hand, turning from the lagoon before them and guiding the stunned doctor back up the slope. "That is The Cannon Master," she said in a hushed tone. "The inscriptions on the pillars foretell his coming, and yet he is as eternal as the moon. He is one who is sentenced to cross his own path."

"What does that mean?" Carl asked in bewilderment.

"It means," Sherrie said with a note of frustration, "that he does not concern you. He is Guardian of The Heorte... you would do well to avoid him and his ilk. Now come on, we need to get clear of here before the cave mouth closes again."

"I don't understand," Carl protested. "Is that it? What happens now?"

Sherrie shrugged and pulled him on. "The terms of your agreement will be honored, and you'll be made the new head of NASA's SETI Program. Administrator Frosch will have your contract ready by the time we return. Cheer up Doctor Sagan... as long as you heed the call, this'll be good for you."

END

NOTES & ACKNOWLEDGEMENTS

If you ever come with me on a night out, I am almost guaranteed to tell you, after a single drink, what a wonderful art writing is, and how everyone should try it.

Give me a couple more drinks, and I will probably tell you that the art of writing has very little to do with the business of publishing. That is not to say that I am not grateful for being where I am, because I really, *really* am... but it is safe to say that it does not look or feel anything like I thought it would.

Publishing has undergone a revolution in the last five years, perhaps akin to what the music industry went through at the end of the nineties with the rise of the internet. There is no well oiled marketing machine behind each of my releases. There is no army of sales men and women selling my work into whatever excellent retail establishment you found this tome in.

Writers are expected to undertake the majority of their own marketing, and if sales do not meet expectations... well then contracts are terminated, and it is back to Square One.

There are hundreds, if not thousands, of authors trying their damndest to sell just one more copy of their book. There are many good writers who just cannot get the exposure they need, and so quit completely, and then there are those who, for one reason or another, see their work catapulted in to the collective consciousness of their respective genres. The difference between failing and succeeding lies with the reader.

All of my success is down to my readers. I really mean that.

If you did not buy my work and tell your friends and family, then I would be just like so many other authors who have written books that have never sold.

At the time of writing this, there are some three thousand fans on my Facebook page, and I have never met the overwhelming majority of you. Yet, over the last two years, we have all developed a strange kinship. We mail each other, swap jokes, share views on the latest movies or TV series… and some of you even let me into your lives to share whatever trials and tribulations you are going through.

To each and every one of you, you have my sincere heartfelt thanks.

The work that you are holding is part payment for that debt of gratitude. The events are largely fictitious, but the characters are real. I have used the names, with permission, of some of my fans, who I have never met yet have got to know so well.

So thank you; Tom Jenkins & his wife Sherrie, Rose Santiago, Adam Cannon & his wife Emma, Andy Tong, Jon Graves, Jason Parrot, and my long time friend, Fred Gustafsson.

And yet the story does not stop there. Beyond these few, there are literally thousands of you who have at one time or another have mailed in to ask a question, pass comment, or just tell me that you are enjoying my work.

So, in no particular order, a big thank you to:

Carol Batters, Anthony Mills, Heather Doricott, Gwyene Redd, James C. Baker, Röd Nelson (hi Other Me!), John Berven, Ján Molnár, John Cumming, Lynsey Hook, Vicky Watts, Sarah Slater, Sylvia Gurr, Martin Locke, Helen Morton, Stewart Dobbie, Ellie Cohen, Buddah Wayne Jackson, Sharon Wann, Mark Quinn, Petros Petrosyan, Emma Willis, William Tooker, Daniel Hill, Al Burrows, Paul Homer, Scott Beard, Valerry Meow, Harry Pearce, Sensei Ellis Amdur, Chris Bennett, Heath McDaniel, Claire Wiltshire, and Natalie Curtis.

Darrell Pitman, Niwde Allidap Zarem, Kylie Townsend, Doug Gelsleichter, Charlotte Bennett (Sis!), Moira Hunter-Liddle, Justin Fitzgerald, David White, James Bridge, Nikki Slack, Martin Newhouse, Piers Groom, Sarah Hale, Aaron Jones, Bruce James Coleman, Trisha Johnson, Edward Hunt, Judy Newlin, Guy Baxendale, Shane Hailey, Margaret Lamb, Mark Demers, Omnipotent Mind, Billy Calloway, Laura Mills, La Bella Reina Earl, Mandy D'Eredita, Amanda Schiffer, Yog Timoth, and Lisa Shavers.

Ankh Iznogood Moody, Alberto De Jesus, Jaiye-ola Akindipe, Christopher DeChello, Tammy Barr Pacenza, , Thorn Da Costa, Kiko Alejo, Benoit St-Laurent, Robert Lawrence, Norman Humphrey, Cindy Jo Conner, Salix Hazel Coleman, Sarah Lane, Audra Rastonis, Anita Milan, Mark Morris, Nicole Montgomery, Marcelo Cecarelli, Ayame Ela Swisher, Jay Rodriguez, Richard Rubalcaba, Jeremiah Lee Keen, Donna Parker-Ross, Frank J Garcia, Luca Parissenti, Israel Martinez, Daemon T. Savage, Fallon Lak, and Lee Paul.

Declan Walker, Sensei Andy Tierney, Charlie Currie, Heather McDaniel, Carlos Roche, Eleanor Thomson, Linda Forret, Stephanie Harris, Amy Fishburn, Hugh Matthews, David Buchanan, Chez Williams, Randall Marks, and last but by no means least, Nelson Davidson.

And of course all the literary pages that have promoted my work. Thank you to all of the admins at Horrorfanz, Twisted Mentality, Horror Books,

Books – An Escape, Viking Scotland, Arts In Fife, and Dunfermline Free Press.

Finally, to my wife for her patience, Graham & Judith for editing, and to Clive Brown for providing technical advice. As ever, if a particular detail is right, credit is due to Clive, and where it is wrong it is down to me.

Once again, and sincerely, thank you all.

Martin

Scotland, December 2013

ABOUT THE AUTHOR

Martin Adil-Smith was born to a Persian mother and an English father in London, 1978. He completed a BA (Hons) in Criminology at Middlesex University in 1999, before pursuing a career in commercial Real Estate.

Martin's literary heroes are Stephen King, HP Lovecraft, and Anne Rice. He is passionate about music, and in particular lesser known acts such as Paradise Lost, Fields of the Nephilim, and Serpico.

He lives in Scotland, with his wife and daughter and when he is not reading or listening to music, he pretends to write.

You can follow The Spirals of Danu at the following social networks:

www.facebook.com/spiralsofdanu
www.twitter.com/spiralsofdanu

Made in the USA
Charleston, SC
03 December 2013